# Star Trek®

# Captain Kirk's

# *Guide to Women*

## How to Romance Any Woman in the Galaxy

## John "Bones" Rodriguez

**Based on *Star Trek*
created by Gene Roddenberry**

POCKET BOOKS

New York    London    Toronto    Sydney

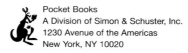

Pocket Books
A Division of Simon & Schuster, Inc.
1230 Avenue of the Americas
New York, NY 10020

This book is published by Pocket Books, a division of Simon & Schuster, Inc., under exclusive license from CBS Studios Inc.

First Pocket Books trade paperback edition February 2008

POCKET and colophon are registered trademarks of Simon & Schuster, Inc.

For information about special discounts for bulk purchases, please contact Simon & Schuster Special Sales at 1-800-456-6798 or business@simonandschuster.com.

Designed by Richard Oriolo

Manufactured in the United States of America

10   9   8   7   6   5   4   3   2   1

ISBN-13: 978-1-4165-4315-2
ISBN-10:      1-4165-4315-5

I dedicate this book to Mark Rodriguez, my first role model.

# contents

# introduction

ATTENTION, MISTER! MY NAME IS BONES RODRIGUEZ.

I'm a *Star Trek* fan, and proud of it! Some would call me a Trekkie, others

would say I am a Trekker, but either way, I am committed to *Star Trek* like

I've been entranced by an Elasian tear. I wrote this book because it is a

well-known fact that many Trekkies have had some difficulties locking their

tractor beams onto members of the fairer sex. While their memory banks

are full of technical aspects of the *Star Trek* universe, including storylines, character names, and verbatim quotes, many have missed the most critical data on romance, and as a result:

## Trekkies Don't Get Chicks.

However, by applying the same impulse-power for technical knowledge to the romantic side of the universe, I believe that Trekkies will transform into the sex symbols of the future. *Star Trek* conventions will be run by "unprincipled, evil-minded, lecherous kulaks," with attendees celebrating *Pon farr* every year. I envision a world where Trekkies are endorsing perfume, jeans, and underwear. I dream of the first Trekkie centerfold, the first Trekkie president, and the first Trekkie sex scandal.

*Captain Kirk's Guide to Women* is not just about smooth pickup lines, torn shirts, and flying leg kicks. Although those tools are as important as logic is to a Vulcan, there are thoughts, attitudes, and ideals that you must replicate if you are going to become a dilithium-powered Don Juan.

This guide is about becoming the type of man who attracts women. But first . . .

# top ten things I learned
## about *love* from *star trek*

1. "Humans are overly preoccupied with the subject of love."

2. "It is a human characteristic to love little animals, especially if they're attractive in some way."

3. "The heart is not a logical organ."

4. "You can learn something from Mister Spock; stop thinking with your glands."

5. "The pleasure is in the learning of each other."

6. "[Love is] the total union of two beings."

7. "Too much of anything, even love, isn't necessarily a good thing."

8. ". . . the things love can drive a man to—the ecstasies, the miseries, the broken rules, the desperate chances, the glorious failures, and the glorious victories."

9. "Love sometimes expresses itself in sacrifice."

10. "Too much love is dangerous; Cupid's arrow kills Vulcans."

And the bonus one:

"Caring for each other, being happy with each other, being good to each other—that's what we call love. You'll like that a lot."

Keep these quotes in mind as we begin your journey to . . .

# Becoming Your Own Captain

**CAPTAIN KIRK IS A LEADER, AND CHICKS DIG LEADERS.**

He is "bright, loyal, fearless, and imaginative." Women see Captain Kirk as

"a man of morality, decency; handsome and strong," and gravitate to him

like a starship with a decaying orbit to a planet. He's his *own captain*. He

stands up for himself even when the evidence is against him. He fights for

what he believes in, even if he's under the influence of mind-controlling

spores. He protects the weak, even if they insist on reporting for their

own execution.

His full-power nature forces him to take action in the wink of an eye, and his force of will has more power than a matter/antimatter reactor.

What about you? You already have all of these traits to different degrees, but maybe you haven't diverted power to them as much as you could. Maybe these are underdeveloped ideas, orbiting around in your mind, and you want to explore them. You're going to learn to:

### Be Your Own Captain

Take this guide and mind-meld with Captain James T. Kirk. Learn from the record tapes and the historical documents. Find your own ship, embark on your own mission, be your own captain. Until you engage those engines, you'll just be another . . .

## Redshirt

In every landing party, there is a mix of personalities: redshirts, crew members, and the captain. (Which one are you? Take our online quiz, "Are you a Redshirt or a Captain?," at www.KirksGuide.com.)

A redshirt's duty is to get killed. His death serves as a warning to the rest of the landing party; his sacrifice lets more valuable crew members and the captain avoid danger. Any danger is usually well hidden until the redshirt pokes his head into something he shouldn't have, or investigates something without backup, or is too eager to start a fight. As clumsy as a three-fingered Tellarite, he is "young and . . . inexperienced."

A redshirt gets killed by flowers.

He is a valuable follower, but ultimately expendable. He steps on exploding rocks and gets in the way of evil ultimate computers. On a romantic mission, he is the one who goes out with the ugly girl. (I think most of us are attracted by beauty and repelled by ugliness—one of the last of our prejudices.) He also may date the walking freezer unit who has on full deflectors, just so the rest of the landing party can have an enterprise incident.

A redshirt gets tongue-tied when speaking to a woman. In this context the term can also be used as a verb, as in, "Dude—she was so beautiful, I totally redshirted."

In the presence of a beautiful woman, we've all been redshirts at one time or another (I know a place where the women are so . . . Do you know the place?). Anyway, you must survive being a redshirt if you want to be promoted to . . .

## Crew Member

A crew member is head of his department. He surveys the terrain for life signs (love signs?), takes tricorder readings, and reports back to the captain. He's loyal, committed, and trustworthy.

Although susceptible to enemy mind-control from Omicron spores or a creature in his body, near-fatal wounds from an Old West shoot-out or a knight's lance, every space sickness in the galaxy—including Rigelian fever, hyper-aging, and xenopolycythemia—he'll be fine and back to normal duty within a week.

On a romance mission, a crew member is also known as your wingman. If you make a standard orbital approach to more than one woman at a time, you will both complement and work with each other. "He is quite capable of

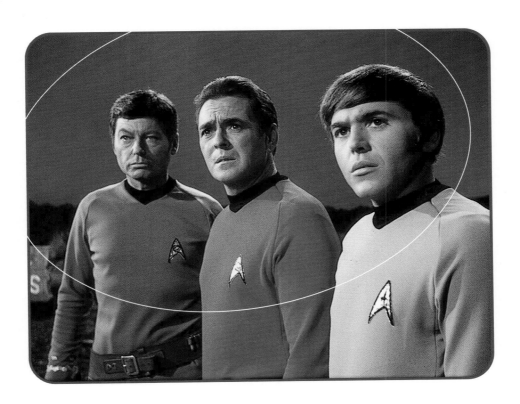

[lady] killing—logically and efficiently." There is no competition between the crew member and the captain, only cooperation.

The crew member may take command and "have the conn" when the captain leaves the ship for any reason. The captain might beam over to an alien vessel or down to an unfamiliar planet, and he's got to know that the crew member will be there to protect the ship.

Captain Kirk relies on his crew members—Spock, McCoy, Scotty, Uhura,

Sulu, and Chekov—to help him perform at his best. Without them, he can't be as effective a captain as he wants to be. And as the mission continues, most of these crew members eventually become . . .

## The Captain

The captain is the leader. "In every revolution, there's one man with a vision." He upholds the vision and directs the mission. He takes full responsibility, and as a result will find whatever options he can to bring about a successful mission. He doesn't blame or criticize, but instead leads by example, by praise, and by appreciation. He trusts himself, and his crew trusts him to do his best for them.

Contrary to popular belief, the captain does *not* need to be a paragon of virtue—on a romantic mission, he may even be the opposite.

However, no one and nothing gets in between a captain and his ship. A "ship" is someone's dream, or someone's goals for their life. Captain Kirk's goals were to spread the ideals of freedom and liberty throughout the galaxy, and his ship was the instrument he did it with—the *Enterprise*.

> KIRK: **If I get my hands on the headquarters genius that assigned me a female yeoman . . .**
>
> McCOY: **What's the matter, Jim, don't you trust yourself?**
>
> KIRK: **I've already got a female to worry about. Her name is *Enterprise*.**

If you are going to *be your own captain,* you must find or choose your "ship." Once you do, you'll begin to tap into your Inner Kirk and rise in the ranks from being an utterly expendable redshirt to becoming your own captain, invulnerable even to a hammering by a Greek god. And who else to model yourself after but the finest captain to ever serve in Starfleet?

## Captain James T. Kirk

Captain Kirk is a leader with a mission. He takes action quickly, and he loves life. Who else would start a war on Eminiar VII just to end a war? He believes in personal freedom, exploration, and love—that's why he destroyed the "god" on Gamma Trianguli VI. Kirk cares about people, and he wants to make the galaxy a better place. No chair-bound paper-pusher would have enough corbomite to kidnap the High Advisor of Ardana to end apartheid. His bold self-confidence comes from trusting himself to take risks, and he believes he is making a difference in the galaxy.

> **If your mission comes first, and you are going somewhere in your life, people will want to follow. That's being your own captain.**

Captain Kirk has a sort of two-men characteristic. Although he has the mysterious public persona of a starship captain, he lets people into his private life in a way that makes them feel special. He knows all of the crew personally (some of them more intimately than others), and takes

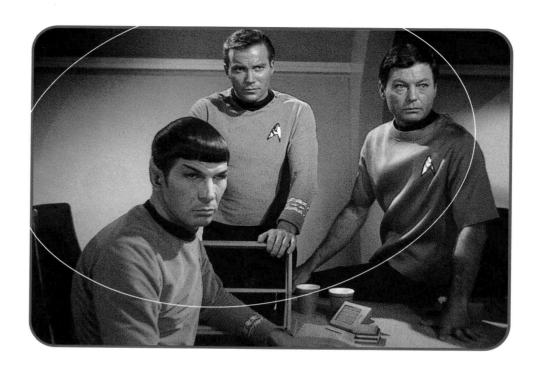

full responsibility for them and their safety. Kirk was once split into an evil side and a good side, and Spock made the following observation:

> "You have here an unusual opportunity to appraise the human mind, or to examine, in Earth terms, the roles of good and evil in a man. His negative side, which you call hostility, lust, violence. And his positive side, which Earth people express as compassion, love, tenderness. And what is it that makes one man an exceptional leader?

"We see here indications that it is his negative side which makes him strong—that his evil side, if you will, properly controlled and disciplined, is vital to his strength."

What we discover later is that his good side has courage. Courage isn't lack of fear, it is acting in spite of it, and it is Kirk's good side that has the control and discipline to take responsibility. Your evil side may go on shore leave to spread your space seed, but it's your good side that has the courage to be the empath and seek your way to Eden.

The captain's mind is always making choices between two opposites: confidence and humility; strength and compassion; action and wisdom; logic and emotion.

As a leader, confidence makes the goal, humility makes the plan. Strength decides, compassion leads. Action starts things, wisdom sees them through. Logic makes a living, emotion makes a life. Kirk has a duty to annihilate alien parasites on planet Deneva, but he refuses to destroy the colonists who are infected.

And in a lover, confidence announces, humility shares. Strength gives, compassion receives. Action moves, wisdom directs. Logic is what, emotion is why.

Kirk depends on his two closest friends and advisors to give him different points of view. Spock, cold as a Gorn, advises him with his Vulcan logic, and Leonard "Bones" McCoy, with a plenitude of human weaknesses, advises him from an emotional-spiritual viewpoint. Kirk takes the opinions and makes the decision—and if it's anything like the no-win scenario of the *Kobayashi Maru,* he figures out a third option.

And you'll need all of the options you can get when you embark on . . .

# The Mission

CAPTAIN KIRK IS A MAN ON A MISSION, LEADING HIS

crew toward the future he is building. He bends the rules when necessary,

and blows up enemies if he has to. Sure, he may have broken the Prime

Directive a few times, wiped out entire species, and changed history along

the way, but his mission for five years remained constant.

You now have a similar mission, but yours may be different from Kirk's. Your

mission duration may be different too. Are you looking for a one-night shore

leave, or are you looking for a long-term assignment? Are you on a mission for conquest, or for love? Your destination might be Utopia Planitia, but you may stop at other spaceports along the way. On the other hand, you may be out one night looking for Orion slave girls and find yourself lost in time with a Goody Two-shoes missionary. By staying the course of your mission, even though you destroy supercomputers, transport to evil mirror universes, or fight alongside Abraham Lincoln, you'll get the girl and be ready for more next week.

Now let's explore the three main objectives of your mission:

1. **To Explore Strange New Worlds**
2. **To Seek Out New Life and New Civilizations**
3. **To Boldly Go Where No Man Has Gone Before**

## Explore Strange New Worlds

Women come from strange new worlds; I've heard that they come from Venus, but that's a gray area. The worlds that women occupy are filled with beauty products, good table manners, and constant, never-ending sharing. They have different rules too. To wear the same outfit as another woman is a violation, and to go to the bathroom alone is social suicide. If you attempt a mind-meld with a woman, you run the risk of being brain damaged and winding up in a wheelchair with a blinking light as your only form of communication.

Despite all of these terrors, you must venture forth, so be prepared. You will need a fully equipped landing party, complete with tricorders to detect female life-forms, universal translators to understand their strange forms of communication ("I have never understood the female capacity to avoid a direct answer to any question"), a few expendable redshirts to be sacrificed, and a couple of trustworthy crew members to bail you out just in case you meet Klingons.

When you're prepared, get out of your normal surroundings and head for different star systems. Explore the female species' habitat. Maybe you'll find love at the Christmas party, in the ship's theater, or in a coed jail. Just keep scanning the quadrants until you get a hail.

But stay alert for whatever happens. Just when you think you are meeting the perfect woman—beautiful, gracious, and brilliant—be aware that she may not be human. She may be a robot. Or an alien. Or a witch. Or a salt-sucking vampire in disguise. Or the daughter of Kodos, the mass murderer who killed thousands.

## Seek Out New Life and New Civilizations

Just like exploring strange new worlds, you will discover new life, new races, new species. Step outside the boundaries of your normal life of 3-D chess, Romulan ale, and engineering manuals. There are entire civilizations out there, like Cygnet XIV, the planet dominated by females, who might love it if you beamed in for a little "oochy-woochy kootchy-koo."

# Boldly Go Where No Man Has Gone Before

This is the *cornerstone* of the Kirk courting agenda:

**Be going, boldly—and make her feel special.**

Leaders have a mission. They are going somewhere—*boldly*—and people want to follow someone like that. If you're some chair-bound paper-pusher going nowhere, no one will follow. But if you are out discovering anomalous phenomena, having adventures, and meeting new species, a woman will think you are "really now."

And since you are going somewhere, *boldly,* when you make time for her, then she is, by association, special too. No man has made her feel that she is interesting, that he wants to know more about her, that he wants to protect her, be her champion, connect with her.

*That's* where no man has gone before!

No man has made her feel that she is the most important, most cherished thing in the galaxy. No man has made her feel that he'd trade an entire dilithium mine for her kiss.

I'm not talking about getting all redshirt on her. I'm talking about being someone special, and making her feel special too. And how do you do that? There are several ways, and we are going to touch on a few of them now:

PLAYING HARD TO GET. **By playing hard to get, you establish that getting your attention is a difficult thing, and if you are awarding her that special attention, then she must be special.**

**BEING TWO MEN.** By having a public persona and a private one, you show that your audience is special to you. By letting someone in, you are awarding the special attention. You can do that by being open to everyone, like Kirk, in which case some people will want to be even more special. Or you can be closed to most, like Captain Pike, and be mysterious.

**PASSIONATE RESPECT AND CARE.** By respecting and caring for all people, you demonstrate that you have an open heart, and women will be drawn to that passion. She'll wonder, if you're passionate about your duties, what else will you be passionate about?

Redshirts don't understand this. They are trying to be just like the other redshirts. "Bonk, bonk on the head!" If you are your own captain, with your own vision and your own mission, then you will attract someone who wants to be a part of that mission.

In short, your mission is to explore, discover, and *act* with *boldness*—to step forward with *confidence* that your mission, whatever it is, will lead to victory, and that *you* are going with or without her. When you believe it, so will she, and she'll want a piece of the action.

## Duties

Every mission has its duties, and there are four stages of any galactic/romantic encounter:

## FIRST CONTACT

Where do you meet, and under what circumstances? Are you the first visitor to her planet, or did you respond to her distress signal? Is she being attacked by humanoid reptiles, or by the space-traveling spirit of Jack the Ripper?

Make your introduction count. Give your name with pride, as if you were representing your entire species. "I am Captain James T. Kirk of the *U.S.S. Enterprise*." It's better than, "Hey, I'm Joe."

What are the customs on her planet? During a first contact, do you bow, shake hands, kiss, or:

> **KIRK: It's the custom of my people to help one another when we're in trouble. [*They kiss.*]**
>
> **SHAHNA: And . . . and this . . . is this . . . also helping?**
>
> **KIRK: You could call it that.**
>
> **SHAHNA: Please . . . help me once again. [*They kiss again.*]**

## BRIEFING

You share information with each other, looking for what you have in common, or what you can talk further about. When Kirk is in briefing mode, he is also thinking about the debriefing. (This is a joke. Get it? Debriefing?)

Does she need to be taught table manners, or is she a coldhearted robot who needs her passion awakened? As you grow more familiar, you can let her in by sharing special moments with her or by letting her call you by a different name ("Call me Jim").

The point of this is to talk about things that interest her, or let her talk about things that interest her, and usually that topic is—you guessed it—*her*.

Briefing can last a lifetime as you share information about each other. Remember, a woman is into constant, never-ending sharing, but a little mystery never hurt anybody.

## ACTION

A captain makes decisions and acts quickly. He knows that a body in motion tends to stay in motion, so even if he makes the wrong decision, the action can be redirected. A redshirt will vacillate and miss an opportunity ("like a door opened, and closed again"). For most people, "A little less analysis, and more action—that's what we need," is excellent advice.

The briefing and action portions of your mission continue for the entire duration of a relationship, as you get closer and more involved in each other's lives. You are constantly evaluating and reevaluating your actions, based on information uncovered, determining whether to induct her into your united federation of mattresses, or abandon her to the Klingons.

## DEBRIEFING

Taking off the underwear (that's the joke if you missed it before). When it's naked time, be a devil in the dark, a turnabout intruder, perform a corbomite maneuver, and make it last until she reaches the city on the edge of forever.

# Captain Kirk

## *"Mr. Lovey-Dovey"*

Captain James T. Kirk: Philanderer of the Future, Light-Speed Lothario, Sci-Fi Swinger. A passionate man, he cares for and respects all life; it doesn't matter whether it is human, alien, or robotic, male or female.

But he likes to kiss the females.

As a plasma-driven playboy, Captain Kirk follows four guiding stars. The following case studies are divided into:

1. **Always Say Yes**
2. **Awaken Her Passion**
3. **Care for Your Exes**
4. **Increase Her Self-Esteem**

Whereas Kirk demonstrates all of these principles in all of his relationships, I will be highlighting the relevant historical documents.

# Always Say Yes

Redshirts who say no are rewarded by the security they feel, and captains who say yes are rewarded by the adventures they have.

Captain Kirk says yes, and he has adventures.

What about you?

If you want the kinds of adventures Captain Kirk has, be prepared to recognize the beauty in every woman and to accept their gifts. By always saying yes, Kirk gives himself the opportunity to pursue one of his duties—to explore strange new worlds. There is something to be explored in every woman, and all of it is strange!

In the following case studies, you'll note that these women are seducing Kirk, and he goes along for the journey. That's just one of the advantages to being the handsome captain of a starship: sometimes they'll just lower their shields and guide your shuttle in.

In fact, you may even be awarded one of them as a gift . . .

*When in Rome . . .*

# Drusilla

SUBJECT: **Drusilla (Lois Jewell)**

AGE: **Old enough**

SPECIES: **Human**

OCCUPATION: **Roman slave**

LESSON: **If the end is near, go out with a bang!**

## special notes

&ast; **Likes to be commanded.**

&ast; **Has never lied to the one who owns her.**

## telltale quotes

&ast; **"I was told to wait for you; provide wine, food, whatever you wish."**

&ast; **"At the first sign of pain, you will tell me?"**

## log

Captured by twentieth-century Romans on the planet 892-IV, Captain Kirk is to be executed in the morning. The emperor gives him the slave Drusilla as a present so that he can have his last hours "as a man." Kirk makes it clear that he doesn't accept bribes, but a gift . . . is in a different column.

Especially a gift wrapped in a skimpy, shiny dress. When she assures Kirk that no one is looking, he accepts. C'mon, wouldn't you?

# Marta

SUBJECT: **Marta (Yvonne Craig)**

AGE: **Old enough**

SPECIES: **Orion**

OCCUPATION: **Patient at penal colony on Elba II; consort to Captain (Lord!) Garth**

LESSON: **Indulge their art.**

## special notes

* **Most beautiful woman on Elba II.**

* **Writes poetry.**

## telltale quotes

* **"Why can't I blow off just one of his ears?"**

* **"No, you mustn't stop me. He's my lover and I have to kill him."**

## log

Marta is green and pretty.

She dances and writes poetry.

Lord Garth's a jerk to our Captain Kirk.

"What's queen to queen's level three?"

*Dude, she wants you for your phasers*

# Nona

**SUBJECT:** **Nona (Nancy Kovack)**

**AGE:** **Mature**

**SPECIES:** **Kahn-ut-tu**

**OCCUPATION:** **Scheming, witch-like wife of Tyree**

**LESSON:** **Women like power, but some women *really* like it.**

## special notes

* **Lady Macbeth has nothing on her.**

* **Her bedside manner includes gyrations and moans.**

* **If a woman summons you to watch her bathe, she probably wants something.**

## telltale quotes

* **"I have *spells* that help me keep you."**

* **"Our souls have been together—he is mine now."**

## log

Nona may be my favorite of the *Star Trek* women. A beautiful, curvy, and ambitious witch. Did I mention the gyrating and moaning? Nona heals Kirk from a fatal wound with a magical *mahko* root, which also bonds him to her psychically. When she notices his phaser, she sees an opportunity to use the weapon to rule.

There are some women who crave power as much as a giant space amoeba. They'll consume it, they'll always be hungry for more, and they'll use whatever methods they can to get it. They'll date a man as ugly as a Medusan, as dumb as a Troglyte, or as heartless as a Vian just to get some status.

It is one thing to be attracted to a man who happens to be powerful, but it is entirely different to love power itself. Although Nona is Tyree's wife, she seduces Kirk, and fully intends to switch sides when she gets the phaser. Marlena Moreau (see page 59) falls into the same category; they both seek out men of power because they feel as empty as negative space without it.

Despite all of the scheming and plotting, Nona gets killed by the other tribe. When you're your own captain, there will be women who are interested in you strictly for your phasers. If a married woman summons you to watch her bathe, maybe you should take evasive action.

But . . . did I mention the gyrating and moaning?

*Summer lovin'*

# Miramanee

SUBJECT: **Miramanee (Sabrina Scharf)**

AGE: **Marrying age**

SPECIES: **Human**

OCCUPATION: **Tribal priestess**

LESSON: **You can be happy if you're a god.**

## special notes

✳ **Doesn't mind proposing to a man.**

✳ **Likes to celebrate "joining day."**

✳ **Wears a sporty headband, but doesn't play handball.**

## telltale quotes

✳ **"I must see to the needs of the god. It is my duty."**

✳ **"Each kiss is as the first."**

## log

Captain Kirk falls into an obelisk on a planet and emerges a god.

All in a day's work.

Although Kirk has amnesia, thinks he's a god, and renames himself
Kirok, he still has his phaser-powered libido. After bringing a boy back from
the dead (as gods do), Kirk is pronounced tribal healer and must be joined
to Miramanee.

The only problem is that she is promised to Salish, who gets very jealous.

Their love lasts for two months—while the *Enterprise* keeps looking for the captain—just like a summer camp fling. Kirk and Miramanee frolic in the woods, make love by the lake, and get married. It's an idyllic happiness.

Have you ever been on vacation and felt as if you had amnesia? As if you became someone else for a little while, and you realy liked that person? Have you ever fallen in love so fast, and felt like you had an entire lifetime romance in the span of a summer? Even shorter? "Kirok" creates a new life; his mission is to expand the village. Miramanee wants to follow, so they get married, and she gets pregnant.

When you have this experience, who will you become? After a weekend fling, what happens on Monday? If you're a god—whatever you want.

*Yeah, but it was a great two minutes!*

# Deela

SUBJECT: **Deela (Kathie Brown)**

AGE: **A few hours**

SPECIES: **Scalosian**

OCCUPATION: **Queen of Scalos**

LESSON: **Fast women, fast times—play hard to get.**

## special notes

✳ **She's fast—if you know what I mean . . .**

✳ **Slips roofies into drinks.**

✳ **Uses her invisibility as a man would; gotta respect that!**

## tell-tale quotes

✳ **"I liked you better before—stubborn, and irritating, and independent."**

✳ **"I want to keep this one a long time; he's pretty."**

✳ **"This species is capable of much affection."**

## log

Deela moves fast. An hour for her is like one of our seconds. She knows what she wants, and goes and gets it. She even kisses Kirk before he can detect it. Women can do that. Men go to jail for that stuff. Kirk just thinks she's an insect buzzing around the ship until she sneaks a roofie into his drink and

hyperaccelerates him to match her speed. When they first meet, before either of them says anything, she kisses him!

Have you ever been brought into a fast woman's world? It's all fun times, parties, and sex. The romance that rockets on the way up crashes even faster on the way down. Similar to a summer fling, except this woman is a little dangerous because you're never the only guy.

Deela has a jealous but obedient husband, Rael. He has to endure Deela's mating with other men from all over the galaxy, and she is unsympathetic to his feelings. She enjoys torturing Rael by flaunting her enjoyment of Kirk in front of him, and she enjoys the danger it means for Kirk. She likes danger.

Deela is a queen among her people, so she of course likes it when Kirk disobeys her by playing hard to get. If a woman is used to getting everything she wants, and then has to actually work for something, her anticipation will build like an overloading phaser and explode all over you.

Although Kirk tries to help Deela and the Scalosians, they are unwilling to stop their kidnapping and forced mating, so he eventually escapes them and then dooms them to extinction. That's a sure way to never see her again.

*I think we'd better use a condom*

# Odona

SUBJECT: **Odona (Sharon Acker)**

AGE: **Legal**

SPECIES: **Gideon**

OCCUPATION: **Daughter, martyr, guinea pig**

LESSON: **Maybe you should get to know her first.**

## special note

 ❋ Isn't into safe sex.

## telltale quote

 ❋ **"Now that we're alone, can you make it last a long, long time?"**

## log

On a seemingly abandoned *Enterprise,* Kirk finds Odona dancing around the ship alone. What he doesn't know is that Odona is using him to contract Vegan choriomeningitis for her planet for population control. This woman actually *wants* a disease from Kirk, and let's face it—he might have several.

Let me take this time to express the importance of condoms. I don't know what viruses, bacteria, or evil spirits we'll find in the twenty-third century, but if you are going to be a warp-drive womanizer, then you'll need to use protection.

Odona is a leader for her people. She has never been sick before, but she bravely does what she can to help her planet. Her mission is to be responsible to her people. Their romance grows even stronger when the truth comes out; Kirk and Odona see the leader in each other.

Get to know each other. You may find that you can share more than Vegan choriomeningitis.

# Awaken Her Passion

On Vulcan, the women are logical. That's the only planet in the galaxy that can make that claim. Everywhere else, women are emotional creatures who need love, attention, caring, and *passion*. But there are some women who have been deprived of these feelings, or never even knew they existed. "What kind of life is that? Not to be loved. Never . . . to have shown love."

She might be so busy with her work that she hasn't focused on her social life. Maybe it's because she's an android, who has never been "programmed to respond in that area." Maybe she's an alien who is only taking human form for the first time.

You know this woman as the glasses-wearing librarian who hides a passionate nature underneath. Or maybe she's the untrusting scientist who . . . hides a passionate nature underneath. *All* women are hiding a passionate nature underneath, and it's your job as a warp-drive wooer to discover it!

Wherever you find women, you'll find one who is looking for an excuse to free her emotions, and looking for someone to explore her feelings with. Give her that permission to be free; give her the opportunity to explore her new emotions, new feelings, new sexuality, and she'll love you forever.

Or hunt you down.

When you meet a woman who seems to have no passion, or who seems shut down, there's only one thing to do—*awaken her passion!*

*Sugar, spice, and duotronic love circuits*

# Andrea

SUBJECT: **Andrea (Sherry Jackson)**

AGE: **Around 4 or 5 years old—in android years**

SPECIES: **Android**

OCCUPATION: **Mechanical geisha**

LESSON: **Even mechanical geishas get jealous.**

## special notes

✳ **Incapable of love . . . or is she?**

✳ **Can be programmed to please men *and* women!**

✳ **Kinky—likes a little bit of slapping mixed in with her kissing . . . and her programming has kinks in it. (That was a joke.)**

## telltale quotes

✳ **"I will kiss you." (Actually means, "Kiss me or die!")**

✳ **"I am now programmed to please you also."**

## log

Captain Kirk goes down to Exo III to find Dr. Roger Korby, Nurse Chapel's fiancé, who has been missing for five years. Dr. Korby is an engineering and computer science genius who luckily survived the terrible freeze on the planet's surface—*or did he?*

We meet Andrea, the android who has been created to . . . keep Dr. Korby company.

In crisscross suspenders.

And programmed to kiss.

While being held captive, Kirk uses the old "get out of jail by kissing her" ploy. And this time the kiss he gives is so powerful, so passionate, so *human,* she almost short-circuits! The experience awakens her passion for Dr. Korby, and even causes her to kill an android version of Kirk when she gets rejected by it.

Andrea is so confused by her newfound emotions that she kills Dr. Korby and herself while embraced in a kiss. So no matter where you are in the galaxy, remember this: *even mechanical geishas get jealous.*

*"Trick or treat?"*

# Sylvia

SUBJECT: **Sylvia (Antoinette Bower)**

AGE: **Unknown**

SPECIES: **Ornithoid**

OCCUPATION: **Junior member of a team of explorers**

LESSON: **Beware of the cat lady.**

## special notes

✳ **Can be *many* women.**

✳ **Likes new sensations.**

✳ **When she gets catty, she gets *catty!***

## telltale quotes

✳ **"To touch, to feel, to understand the idea of luxury—I like it!"**

✳ **"I come from a world without sensation as you know it. It excites me—I want more."**

## log

Captain Kirk and the crew are being held captive by Sylvia, an ornithoid who finds pleasure in the new human form she has taken. In order to escape, Kirk gives her more pleasure.

However, by awakening her desire for love and passion, Kirk also taught her what anger, rejection, jealousy, and revenge are. Hell hath no fury like a woman scorned, and Sylvia becomes a giant cat, chasing Kirk, Spock, and McCoy through the castle.

You know the cat lady: she's single, lonely, and maybe a little bitter. She has a houseful of cats, and although they keep her company, she longs for a man.

Maybe a little too much.

A cat lady has probably been sexy, vivacious, and loved, and if you awaken those dormant feelings in her, she will rain down love and appreciation on you.

But don't cross her.

At first Kirk pretends to care for her, discusses what she wants, makes her feel special, and talks about a future together. But when she realizes she's being used, the entire landing party has to escape the claws of one giant, angry space pussycat.

*Beware of the cat lady.*

She may seem accommodating, and willing to change anything in her life just to please you, but you'll end up being either a mind-controlled thrall or a mouse caught in a trap!

# Rayna Kapec

**SUBJECT:** **Rayna Kapec (Louise Sorel)**

**AGE:** **Unknown**

**SPECIES:** **Android**

**OCCUPATION:** **Student on Holberg 917G**

**LESSON:** **You can love her, but you can't control her.**

## special notes

 ✳ **Has 15 deactivated twin sisters.**

 ✳ **Has the equivalent of 17 university degrees in science and the arts, loves to waltz, and is a pool shark.**

## telltale quotes

 ✳ **"At last I have seen other men!"**

 ✳ **"I choose where I want to go. What I want to do. I choose. I choose. No. Do not order me. No one can order me!"**

## log

The 6,000-year-old Flint introduces his student Rayna, who has never seen other men before. After some discussion, a game of billiards, and a waltz, Kirk falls in love with her (doesn't take much sometimes). When he gives her one of those full-body kisses, one of Flint's killer-robots enters and almost kills Kirk. Flint orders Rayna away, but being a champion for freedom, Kirk doesn't like it. He offers to take Rayna with him:

**KIRK: Come with me; I offer you happiness.**

**RAYNA: But there is security here.**

**KIRK: You love me—not Flint.**

Rayna is confused by her conflicting emotions because she is an android, built by Flint. "He has created the perfect woman. Her only flaw: she's not human." As the two men she loves fight over her future, she makes her own choice, short-circuits, and dies. "The joys of love made her human, and the agonies of love destroyed her."

You can love her, but you can't control her.

*"Sorry" never felt so good!*

# Kelinda

SUBJECT: **Kelinda (Barbara Bouchet)**

AGE: **Unknown**

SPECIES: **Kelvan, but in human form**

OCCUPATION: **Traveler, usurper, apology accepter**

LESSON: **Forgive, forget, fool around.**

## special notes

* **Likes flowers.**

* **In her true form, has hundreds of arms—the better to touch you with.**

## telltale quotes

* **"Why do you build such mystique around a simple biological function?"**

* **"Very odd creatures, these humans."**

## log

Kelinda is a Kelvan. Kelvans conspire to conquer us curious creatures who can be configured into cubes and crushed. Kirk crumbles at the conclusion.

Hanar, with high haughtiness, heinously handicaps our heroes by halting the human hull headquarters.

But the crew concocts a kind of cooperative conspiracy.

Scotty takes Tomar, and toasts with totally toxic tonics.

But Kelinda the Kelvan is cute, so Kirk kisses the Kelvan Kelinda, and Rojan refuses to rethink revenge.

The plan produces a pretty peculiar product.

Instead of injuring invaders, we welcome wonderful friends to the Federation family.

# Care for
# Your Exes

Captain Kirk doesn't make enemies of his exes. He loved them once, therefore they must be good people. A captain never stops caring, and always wants the best for his exes; just because it didn't work out between you doesn't mean you can't remain friends.

Or at least civil.

Whether she is just someone you hooked up with at the Christmas party, someone who's prosecuting you for murder, or someone who's trying to switch bodies with you, kill you, and steal your identity, remain forever courteous, like Kirk.

*Remember that time?*

# Dr. Helen Noel

SUBJECT: **Dr. Helen Noel (Marianna Hill)**

AGE: **Old enough**

SPECIES: **Human**

OCCUPATION: **The best assistant Kirk has ever "had"**

LESSON: **Sometimes they just want a piece of the action.**

## special notes

❋ **Invite her to all Christmas parties.**

❋ **Doctor of penology and psychiatry.**

## telltale quote

❋ **"Perhaps it'd be simpler if you called me Helen?"**

## log

Dr. Helen Noel is assigned to assist Kirk in his investigation of a mental hospital. When she appears in the transporter room, she has a sly look in her eye, and Kirk is a little taken aback. It's implied that they got together during the Christmas party.

The one-night Christmas stand?

She assumes a lot of familiarity based on their past history, but Kirk wants to keep it all business:

HELEN: **Perhaps it'd be simpler if you called me Helen?**

KIRK: **This is another time, another place, another situation.**

While they are investigating the facility, they discover a neural neutralizer that can erase someone's memories and replace them. While innocently experimenting with the neural neutralizer, Dr. Helen rewrites the memory in Kirk's mind and reveals that she wanted him to be *more* aggressive! Eventually, Kirk is captured and mind-controlled into loving her passionately.

*And she doesn't like it.*

The lesson? Sometimes they just want a piece of the action.

You'll find that although you can show a woman the leader you are, and make her feel special, and be her champion, sometimes they just want some action, so you can skip the first three duties and go right on to the debriefing. (This is the taking-off-the-underwear joke that you've now read three times. Is that enough?)

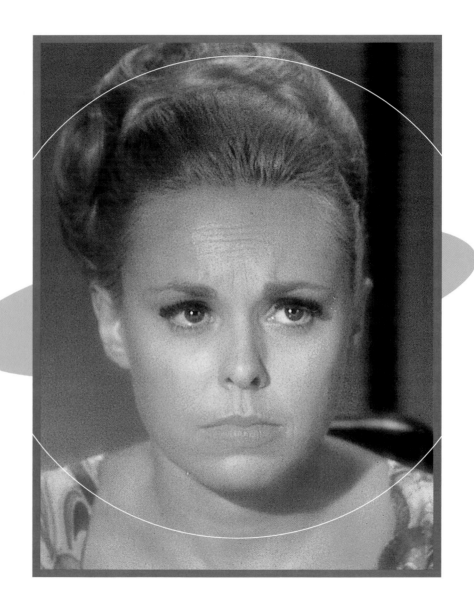

# Dr. Janet Wallace

SUBJECT: **Dr. Janet Wallace (Sarah Marshall)**

AGE: **Unknown**

SPECIES: **Human**

OCCUPATION: **Endocrinologist**

LESSON: **Pity sex is no sex at all.**

## special note

❋ **Likes older men.**

## telltale quotes

❋ **"Be a little less the cool, efficient captain, and a little more the old friend."**

❋ **"I see Captain James Kirk: a man of morality, decency, handsome and strong."**

## log

Captain Kirk is suffering from extreme old age and growing older by the minute—much older. He sees his old flame Janet, and they recount why they broke up. "You have your career, and I have my ship, and neither one of us will change." It would seem to end there, but Janice has been left a widow recently by a man who was twenty-six years her senior. So, she likes old guys, and Kirk is getting older by the minute. What seems like a perfect match is actually rebuffed by Kirk because he is beginning to feel less confident. "What are you offering me, love or a going-away present?" He is unmoved by her advances, as he knows they cannot be together. This would seem to violate "Always say yes." Heh, but—maybe he's maturing by the minute too.

So this is a *crucial* lesson for dealing with women:

**Pity sex is no sex at all.**

And a hallway is a stupid place to hang a mirror.

*Courting the enemy*

# Areel Shaw

SUBJECT: **Areel Shaw (Joan Marshall)**

AGE: **Mature**

SPECIES: **Human**

OCCUPATION: **A very good lawyer**

LESSON: **Duty first; respect her ship.**

## special note

✳ **Is a sucker for flattery.**

## telltale quote

✳ **"Jim Kirk, my dear old love—I *am* the prosecution, and I have to do my very best to have you slapped down hard, broken out of the service in disgrace."**

## log

Captain Kirk's former love Areel Shaw is prosecuting him for murder! She *must* do her best. He respects that. They respect that in each other. Respect her ship!

*Who wears the pants in this relationship?*

# Dr. Janice Lester

SUBJECT: **Dr. Janice Lester (Sandra Smith)**

AGE: **Thirtysomething**

SPECIES: **Human**

OCCUPATION: **Doctor of . . . science**

LESSON: **Like women who like themselves.**

## special notes

* Loves Kirk.

* Hates Kirk.

* Wants to be Kirk.

* Wants to kill Kirk.

## telltale quotes

* "The year we were together at Starfleet was the only time in my life I was alive."

* "It's better to be dead than to live alone in the body of a woman."

## log

Dr. Janice Lester wants to be a starship captain like her ex-lover Kirk, but unfortunately, Starfleet doesn't allow women to be captains.

Wait—huh?

But what about . . . ?

Okay, forget it. Whatever.

Anyway, Janice uses alien technology to switch their life energies. Her plan was then to kill her own body with Kirk in it, and stay as Captain Kirk so she could command the *Enterprise*. It almost works, but eventually she is caught, and the energies are switched back.

You know women like this—their intense hatred for their own womanhood makes living with them impossible. Although she suffers in a sexist society (but wait—I thought . . . okay, forget it), her resentment eats away all of the love she could have shared. Kirk may have awakened her passion, but now she's as resentful as a Klingon.

Her anger prevents her from seeing that Dr. Arthur Coleman loves her. And what does it say about Coleman that he's in love with a woman who wants to be a man?

If you're dating a woman who hates not only herself but her entire gender, stay away as if she were tetralubisol poison. Even though she tries to kill him, Kirk cares for her when she has a breakdown.

# Increase Her Self-Esteem

Everyone has a self-image, and it affects our entire lives. It affects the way we talk, walk, eat, love, and sell fake patents to our mothers. If we believe in our own worth, we'll value ourselves more highly. If we like ourselves, other people will too.

Sometimes we get our self-esteem from the way we think other people see us, and Kirk makes these women feel special by giving them the attention they want. To them, his affection is like food to a starving man, and they respond with love.

Or a battle-ax.

Demonstrating your high regard for someone is an act of love, and Kirk does that for everyone. Great leaders do that. The women in this lesson need someone to hold a mirror up to them: one woman has given up on finding a partner, one has only been with a tyrant, one only knows how to fight, and one has always gotten her way.

You've encountered women like this; maybe she has her defenses up and is always ready to fight, or maybe she's a spoiled brat who is desperately lonely. She may seem harmless enough, just like the sand-bats of Manark-4, who appear to be inanimate rock crystals—until they attack.

A redshirt might treat them the same way other redshirts treat them, but a captain understands human nature. And alien nature. And robot nature . . .

*One out of three? Good odds!*

# Eve McHuron

SUBJECT: **Eve McHuron (Karen Steele)**

AGE: **Older than she seems; marrying age**

SPECIES: **Human**

OCCUPATION: **Professional wife-for-hire**

LESSON: **You either believe in yourself, or you don't.**

## special notes

* Has self-worth issues.
* Can survive sandstorms, cook, clean the kitchen, and never break a nail.
* Has a penchant for lonely, isolated, overworked, rich men.
* Has never met a paragon of virtue.

## telltale quotes

* "We've got men willing to be our husbands!"
* "Why don't you just run a raffle, and the loser gets me!"
* "The sound of the male ego—you travel halfway across the galaxy, it's still the same song."

## log

Harry Mudd has taken it upon himself to recruit wives for settlers, and Eve has enlisted his help to find her a husband. It turns out that the women are actually all ugly, but have used a special Venus drug that enhances the beauty that one already has.

And adds soft lighting.

And does their hair.

Eve is looking to be a help to someone—to "cook, sew, cry, and need"—but has given up because she has decided that men just want someone "selfish, vain, useless." She begins to like Captain Kirk, who sees her value as a person. That a man with duty, honor, and courage—a man with a *mission*—sees her as worthy means a lot to her.

Here's a good tip: if you walk into your room, and a gorgeous woman is in your bed waiting for you—don't act *too* surprised. You might even want to act like it happens all the time.

Captain Kirk shows that he can appreciate Eve for her character and her spirit, not just her beauty, and she likes it.

Just when she starts thinking about staying with Kirk, Harry Mudd has some wise words for Eve: "You'll find out ship's captains are already married to their vessels, girl. You'd find out the first time you come between him and the ship."

Instead, she is tricked into taking a placebo Venus drug and learns the best lesson in all of the *Star Trek* universe:

*You either believe in yourself, or you don't.*

*The girl from the other side of the multiverse*

# Marlena Moreau

SUBJECT: **Lieutenant Marlena Moreau (Barbara Luna)**

AGE: **Experienced**

SPECIES: **Human**

OCCUPATION: **Captain's woman**

LESSON: **Show her a vision of a life she wants, and she'll try to get it.**

## special notes

* Hangs out in the captain's quarters.
* Can use alien technology.
* Likes evil Kirk and our Kirk.

## telltale quotes

* "If I'm to be the woman of a Caesar, shouldn't I know what you're up to?"
* "I've been a captain's woman, and I like it!"

## log

Captain Kirk, Dr. McCoy, Scotty, and Uhura are accidentally transported to a parallel universe where hostility is rewarded and cruelty is the norm.

When Kirk walks in and finds Marlena sleeping in his bed, he doesn't act *too* surprised (see page 58). He learns that they are a couple, and that she is his confidante in this universe.

Evidently, even evil Kirk gets chicks.

Marlena reveals that although the captain hasn't been romantic with her in a while, he used to be, despite being a murderous tyrant. Even evil Kirk knows to "let her in."

Our Kirk shows her compassion, even love, by showing her his vision. Just like he did with Shahna, he raises Marlena's level of thinking and gives her a standard to reach.

Marlena wants to leave with Kirk; she chooses compassion over everything. Instead Kirk gives the mirror Spock and Marlena the idea that together they can change the future.

*Someone needs Gamblers Anonymous*

# Shahna

SUBJECT: **Shahna (Angelique Pettyjohn)**

AGE: **Unknown**

SPECIES: **Human enough**

OCCUPATION: **Drill thrall**

LESSON: **In a battle of the sexes, fight with love.**

## special notes

＊ **Can kick your ass.**

＊ **Wears the same thing every day, even if she works out in it.**

＊ **Likes to be helped; does *not* like to be lied to.**

## telltale quotes

＊ **"I will provide your nourishment."**

＊ **"What is 'beautiful'?"**

＊ **"Please help me once again."**

## log

Captain Kirk, Chekov, and Uhura are kidnapped to a planet where they are forced to battle aliens to support The Providers' gambling habits. They are each given drill thralls who train them to fight: Uhura gets a man, Chekov gets a . . . something, and Kirk gets Shahna.

Big green hair and a teeny-tiny silver outfit. Beautiful.

But she doesn't even know what beautiful is! Kirk teaches her about a better life and tells her about the wonders of the galaxy—he expands her mind and makes her feel special.

He is *going, boldly.*

> KIRK: **It is the custom of my people to help one another when we're in trouble. [*They kiss.*]**
>
> SHAHNA: **Is this also helping?**
>
> KIRK: **You could call it that.**
>
> SHAHNA: **Please help me once again. [*They kiss.*] You have made me feel strangely.**

That's when he makes his escape plan and offers her something else: a right hook.

Shahna had never thought for herself, had never seen compassion. She didn't see that right hook either. She does not appreciate being lied to, and almost kills Kirk.

You have met women like Shahna before: a woman who is used to fighting and having the world be a struggle. Shahna doesn't know about love and caring, or "helping," so Kirk shares his vision of life with her.

In the battle of the sexes, fight with love!

*Dealing with a princess*

# Elaan

SUBJECT: **Elaan (France Nuyen)**

AGE: **Marrying age**

SPECIES: **Elasian**

OCCUPATION: **Dohlman of Elas—whatever that means**

LESSON: **Spoiled brats need a spanking.**

## special note

❋ **Women's tears—weapons in *any* part of the galaxy.**

## telltale quotes

❋ **"Permission to speak was not given."**

❋ **"I did not give you permission to leave!"**

❋ **"I love you. I have chosen you. And still I don't understand why you didn't fight the Klingon."**

## log

This relationship is a twist on self-esteem in that Elaan thinks *too* highly of herself, and has no respect for other people. She is a dohlman (a big deal, apparently), and it makes her impossible to bear. She barks orders at everyone, and is impatient, uncaring, and extremely self-centered.

A total bitch.

Fortunately, Captain Kirk says what everyone else won't: "That's another one of your problems; nobody's told you that you're an uncivilized savage, a vicious child in a woman's body, an arrogant monster."

It turns out that her bitchiness comes from her loneliness as a leader. She just needed someone to care for her genuinely, which Kirk eventually does.

However, he doesn't fall for her until he is affected by her tears—which are a *super love potion!*

The tears of a woman are weapons in any galaxy, in any time period. I have never heard of a man who can stand it when there's a woman crying. I think it is hard-wired in us to care, and do whatever it takes to stop it.

Elaan truly loves Kirk because he had the courage to help her and her mission. Elaan doesn't want to give herself away to another man, but through Kirk's example, she learns that her duty to her people comes first. We hate her at the beginning, and we like her a bit by the end.

I'm kinda disappointed there was no spanking.

# Special
## Considerations

This section contains examples of Captain Kirk falling in love. It also contains a section where he imparts some of his wisdom about women to Charlie X.

*Getting a missionary into missionary*

# Edith Keeler

SUBJECT: **Edith Keeler (Joan Collins)**

AGE: **Sophisticated**

SPECIES: **Human**

OCCUPATION: **Missionary at a twentieth-century mission; "slum angel"**

LESSON: **Stick to your mission, whatever the cost.**

## special notes

✳ **A missionary who never talks about God, but can see the future.**

✳ **Doesn't look both ways when crossing the street.**

## telltale quote

✳ **"A lie is a poor way to say hello."**

## log

Let me make this one thing clear—James T. Kirk was *in love* with Edith Keeler. It's a big debate whether or not she was "the one." The point is this—Kirk was almost willing to destroy the future to save her.

Almost.

Captain Kirk meets Edith Keeler in a very shady way. He and Spock are hiding from the law, and she decides to take them in. Edith is a missionary, and believes that people should be given a chance to prove their worth and contribute to society.

"Now, I don't pretend to tell you how to find happiness and love, when every day is a struggle to survive. But I do insist that you do survive, because the days and the years ahead are worth living for!"

Kirk falls in love with her because they are very similar. She too has a *mission:* to bring people out of the gutter to become contributing members of society. She is an optimist, and sees a future where "men will harness great energies and travel long distances." She is a leader in her community, and just as his leadership is attractive, so is hers.

Her determination and her spirit are what Kirk falls in love with. We don't get to see how their relationship grows, we just see that they spend a lot of time together. He talks to her intimately and enjoys her company.

Unfortunately, Kirk learns that Edith Keeler must die if the future is going to continue as it is supposed to, with the Earth saved from Hitler's forces. Kirk wrestles with his priorities, but in the end not only does he not save her, he even prevents McCoy from doing it—securing the future, but breaking his own heart.

*Don't destroy the world for your woman.*

Besides, she may come back as that bitch from *Dynasty*!

*How to deal with "Daddy's little girl"*

# Lenore Karidian

**SUBJECT:** Lenore Karidian (Barbara Anderson)

**AGE:** 19

**SPECIES:** Human

**OCCUPATION:** Actress with the Karidian Company

**LESSON:** Don't get in between a father and his daughter.

## special notes

* Hides psychotic obsession with Daddy until it's too late.

* Knows how to quote Shakespeare appropriately for real-life situations.

* Artsy chicks can be forward and are given to wildly obvious sexual innuendo.

## telltale quotes

* "This ship has all this power . . . surging and throbbing—yet under control. Are *you* like that, Captain?"

* "But you're safe now, Father—I've saved you!"

## log

Captain Kirk meets Lenore Karidian at a party for the theater company, and *introduces* himself by his title, giving himself a little status, saying it with pride. Notice how gallant he is—offering *his* drink, offering *her* a seat, an opening to begin a *briefing*.

During their conversation, he admires her performance—complimenting something specific about her. He comments how impressed he was, indicating that he is not easily impressed—playing hard to get. When she fishes for the compliment, he immediately assumes she is interested, and takes *action* by leaving the party so they can be alone.

Now comes the two-men conversation, when she notices how different he is in public and in private. Again, it is crucial that a woman *feel special,* and one way to do that is to *let her in*. If you are one way in public, and another in private, with her—that is a sign that you have let her in, and therefore must mean that she is special.

Lenore feels *so* special, in fact, that they lean into each other, and just when they're about to kiss . . .

**Dead Body.**

Forced to postpone the first kiss (you can't have a first kiss in front of a dead body), Kirk arranges for a second meeting with Lenore to continue briefing . . . and maybe some *action*.

At their next meeting, Lenore sees Kirk on the bridge, where his *mission* is headquartered, where his life's work is centered. He is confident, in control, and relaxed; he flirts with her some more.

LENORE: **If we ever needed a Good Samaritan.**

KIRK: **What do you have to trade?**

*That* is a great hard-to-get line. A redshirt would have said, "Oh, okay—*anything* for you." Instead Kirk gives a flirty, playful, interested answer. It's not a yes or a no. It is a *third option*.

Later, they continue briefing:

> **LENORE:** **Did you order the soft light?**
>
> **KIRK:** **If I had ordered soft lights, I'd also have arranged for music and flowers.**
>
> **LENORE:** **Tell me about women in your world.**
>
> **KIRK:** **I'd rather talk about you.**

He shows her that he is interested in *her*—that *she* is special, and that their conversation surrounds *her*.

Toward the end of the episode, when she is having her "I'm cuckoo for Kodos" breakdown, Lenore asks if Kirk was just using her—and out of *respect,* he's truthful: "In the beginning." He reveals that he truly did *care for her*.

Then she tries to kill him, kills her daddy instead, spouts some Shakespeare, and goes to prison . . .

Another *crucial* lesson for dealing with women: *Don't get in between a father and a daughter.*

Especially if she's psycho.

*The "in case of emergency" girl*

# Janice Rand

SUBJECT: **Janice Rand (Grace Lee Whitney)**

AGE: **It's complicated, but let's say 21.**

SPECIES: **Human**

OCCUPATION: **Yeoman**

LESSON: **Don't vent the warp plasma where you breathe.**

## special notes

 ✳ **Best yeoman Kirk ever had.**

 ✳ **Smells like a girl.**

 ✳ **Can be in the captain's quarters when he's not.**

## telltale quotes

 ✳ **"When you mentioned the feelings we'd been hiding, and you started talking about us . . ."**

 ✳ **"I used to try to get you to look at my legs. Captain, look at my legs."**

## log

Yeoman Janice Rand began her career in Starfleet as Captain Kirk's yeoman, performing clerical and administrative duties in very short skirts. She developed a crush on him, but Captain Kirk never approaches her romantically. They maintain a professional relationship (except for a jealous look Rand throws at Lenore Karidian) throughout their careers, because you *don't vent the warp plasma where you breathe.*

When Captain Kirk is split in half, his evil half goes to her quarters and almost assaults her. "You're too beautiful to ignore . . . not anymore . . . We've both been pretending too long. Stop pretending. Let's stop pretending. Come here, Janice."

She is the "in case of emergency" girl, and you only break the glass when you have no other options, and there can be no consequences. When you're a captain, there are women who are waiting for you to need them.

"Then he kissed me and he said that we . . . that he was the captain, and he could order me. I didn't know what to do."

Notice that it's Kirk's evil side who tries to seduce her—the side that actually has no respect for her and doesn't care for her. Kirk's evil side has no thoughts for the future, but his good side understands that his mission must come first. Everyone has an "in case of emergency" girl. She's the friend who likes you but whom you never hook up with—until you can blame it on your "evil" side.

# U.S.S. ENTERPRISE NCC-1701

**SUBJECT:** *U.S.S. Enterprise* **(built in San Francisco Yards)**

**AGE:** **20**

**SPECIES:** *Constitution*-**class**

**OCCUPATION:** **Starship**

**LESSON:** **It's like the first time you fall in love. You never love a woman quite like that again.**

## special notes

＊ **A fast ship.**

＊ **Destroyed and resurrected as NCC-1701-A.**

## telltale quotes

＊ **SHIP'S COMPUTER: Computed and recorded, dear.**

＊ **KIRK: Computer, you will not address me in that manner. Compute.**

＊ **SHIP'S COMPUTER: Computed . . . dear!**

## log

Captain Kirk first met the *Enterprise* in 2264, and he and the *Enterprise* had a twenty-two-year-long relationship. They were both on the same mission, and Kirk had to destroy the *Enterprise* when she was boarded by the Klingons.

He could never allow his true love to be taken by those Klingon bastards. She finally had to give her life in a self-destruct sequence to save the crew and the captain.

By respecting each other, and caring for the same goals and the same people, Captain Kirk and the *Enterprise* had a very successful relationship.

# top *pickup lines* from
## the twenty-third century

1. I am for you.

2. I must touch you; it is my existence.

3. To [NAME], the loveliest human ever to grace a starship.

4. [NAME], be serious, you're not an ordinary human, you're a starship captain.

5. A last tender moment, for you to end your usefulness.

6. I offer you more than you've ever imagined in your wildest dreams. You'll inspire the universe. All men will revere you, almost as a god. And I shall love you for time without end, worlds without end. You shall complete me, and I you.

7. You left us. The room became lonely.

8. There is no one else in my mind, or in my heart.

9. I've never seen perfection, but no woman could come closer to it.

10. When I see you, I . . . I feel like I'm hungry . . . all over.

11. You're too beautiful to ignore. Too much woman.

12. What are you offering me? Love or a going-away present?

13. You're food to a starving man.

14. A meeting of the minds is all very well, but what about love, [NAME]? You're young, attractive, and human.

15. You must realize we are not here by accident; some force, some intelligence, has arranged this . . . for a purpose.

16. Why do you build such mystique around a simple biological function?

# what *not* to do

What would it be like to be a seventeen-year-old boy and never to have seen a woman?

Poor Charlie Evans (aka Charlie X) is in that situation, and he's hornier than a *mugato*. Not only are his hormones on red alert, he also has some incredible power to manifest things out of thin air and to send people away to oblivion.

If not for his superhuman powers, Charlie would be a redshirt. He has no mission (other than getting under Yeoman Rand's skirt). He doesn't care for people unless he needs something from them, and he is miserable unless he's controlling other people. Charlie is impatient and easily offended, but has the power to blow up the ship.

Not attractive. Pretty scary.

There are so many guys like this—and we have all been there—where we want one particular woman so much that nothing else matters. He's like the guy at the bar at closing time who is trying desperately to hook up. Charlie doesn't play hard to get, and he dotes too much on Rand. He tries to impress Rand by giving her flowers and doing card tricks, but they're childish pleas for attention. Of course, these desperate hailing frequencies act as a warning buoy for her to stay away. Desperation isn't sexy.

Remember that this guide is about Becoming Your Own Captain, someone who has a mission and a vision, which attracts women to you.

If you find yourself feeling like Charlie X, reflect on Captain Kirk's advice: "You go slow. You be gentle. I mean, it's not a one-way street, you know, how you feel and that's all. It's how the girl feels too. Don't press, Charlie. If the girl feels anything for you at all, you'll know it.

"She's not the girl, Charlie. The years are wrong, for one thing, and there are other things.

"Charlie, there are a million things in this universe you can have and there are a million things you can't have. It's no fun facing that, but that's the way things are.

"Hang on tight and survive. Everybody does.

"Everybody, Charlie. Me too."

Even though his blood is boiling like a Vulcan during the *Pon farr,* Charlie dismisses the young Tina Lawton and is rude to her in front of Rand. *Never be rude to her friends!* And by the way . . .

"Uh, there are things you can do with a lady, uh, Charlie, that you . . . Uh, there's no right way to hit a woman. I mean, man to man is one thing, but, um, man and woman, uh, it's, uh . . . is, uh . . . Well, it's, uh, another thing. Do you understand?"

You may be a foreigner, be really young, and have superpowers, but you still can't let your desperation overwhelm you.

# graduation and commencement

## Your Own Episode

Cadet, we have researched, studied, and broken down many of the encounters of Captain Kirk. We have been with him during his successes and his few failures. We have risked with him, we have won with him, and we have lost with him. And now it is time for us to leave the bridge of his ship and graduate to our own leadership position.

*You are now your own captain.*

It is now up to *you* to lead your crew to victory. It is up to *you* to create your own identity, to conduct your own missions, to perform your own duties. As you explore strange new worlds, seek out new life and new civilizations, there will be risk, and it is up to you to *boldly* go where no man has gone before.

Take what you have learned here and star in your own adventures, in your own romances. We have learned what the captain has taught us, but there is no teacher like experience. That is why I am *personally* giving you your first mission:

On the next page, you will have the opportunity—as your first command—to:

*Boldly write your own episode!*

# YOUR episode

*Now that you're your OWN captain*
   *You went somewhere, met someone, and had an adventure!*

" _____ "

SUBJECT: _____

AGE: _____

SPECIES: **Human?**

OCCUPATION: _____

LESSON: _____

## special notes

✳ _____

✳ _____

✳ _____

## telltale quotes

✳ " _____ "

✳ " _____ "

✳ " _____ "

So you risked—and you either won or you learned. There is no failure in your mission, and there are many more missions to come. And you didn't do it alone. You can join other captains from all over the world on our Internet site, www.KirksGuide.com, where you can chat, compare notes, and post to forums. You can download more episode forms and tell us about your missions, and your episodes. Sign up for our special events and learn more as we explore the world of dating.

We'll see you around the galaxy!

**acknowledgments**

I can't believe I am actually writing this book. No wonder I am www.TheLuckiestGuyOnThePlanet.com. I am living my dream right now, and I have so many people to thank for it!

Let me first thank my big cousin Mark Rodriguez for introducing me to *Star Trek* and sci-fi; my father, E. John Rodriguez, for also fostering my love for *Star Trek,* and for being his own captain; my mother, Yolanda Escollies, for encouraging me to reach for the stars by reaching herself; and Leonor Rodriguez, for her understanding support.

I have to thank my beautiful, wonderful wife, Laura Valpey Rodriguez, for being the best cheerleader, partner, and love I could ever imagine. Thank you for loving me in tragedy and in comedy. May I give you the love you want and make your time beautiful.

To Rick Kiley, for being my best redshirt, crew member, and captain; let's have more missions and continue boldly going.

To Dave Viscomi, for the adventures I hope we continue to have.

Thank you, Mollie Glick at the Jean Naggar Agency, for seeing the vision of the book and dealing with my two Gemini halves. Thanks to Margaret Clark at Pocket Books for being so calm during my red alerts.

I, of course, have to thank "The Great Bird of the Galaxy," Gene Roddenberry, for creating *Star Trek* and Captain Kirk, and for giving us all a vision of a possible future. Thank you, Majel Barrett, for being his Number One.

To CBS, Paramount, and Simon & Schuster for keeping *Star Trek* going.

To the cast of *Star Trek*—thank you for bringing your characters to life so we feel for them, care for them, and adventure with them on the screen. Thank you for your continued indulgence of us crazies. My hope is to one day play such wonderful characters that inspire people to be their best also.

To William Shatner, for being a personal inspiration and an icon for perseverance, success, and accomplishment. A successful actor, director, author, recording artist (can I say singer?), and philanthropist. If you are unaware of your contribution, let me make it plain: you have inspired millions to better our society by bettering themselves.

To Alex Goldberg, Lesley McBurney, Christina Nicosia, Matt Kalman, Laura Valpey, and Ean Sheehy—thank you for being hilarious.

To the many other people who have inspired me—Oprah Winfrey, Robert Kiyosaki, Tony Robbins, Dennis Kimbro, Joe Vitale, Bob Proctor, Allan Loy McGinnis, Mark Victor Hansen, Suze Orman, Jack Canfield, Donald Trump, Robert Allen, Joe Sugarman, T. Harv Eker, Nido Quebein, John Gray, Jim Stovall, Les Brown, Tom Wood, Randy Gage, Eric Worre, Sean and Marla Cross, Rasul and Heather Davis, Lindsey Hammond, Perry Marshall, Leslie Becker, Bill Gates, Warren Buffett, Richard Branson, Seth Godin, Steven Covey, Miguel de Cervantes, Stuart Wilde, Buckminster Fuller, Paul Zane Pilzer, Ayn Rand, and whoever inspired them.

And of course, thank you to my fellow Trekkers, Trekkies, geeks, dorks, nerds, egghead weirdos, Bronx Science graduates, Skidmore studs, and the ladies who love us. Let your light so shine before men, live long and prosper, *Qapla',* and boldly go where no man has gone before.